# MOLE HILL

## Alex Latimer

# For Lily and Isla

**OXFORD**
UNIVERSITY PRESS

Great Clarendon Street, Oxford OX2 6DP

Oxford University Press is a department of the University of Oxford.
It furthers the University's objective of excellence in research, scholarship,
and education by publishing worldwide. Oxford is a registered trade mark of
Oxford University Press in the UK and in certain other countries

Text and illustration copyright © Alex Latimer 2020

The moral rights of the author and artist have been asserted

Database right Oxford University Press (maker)

First published 2020
British Library Cataloguing in Publication Data available

ISBN: 978-0-19-277256-5
1 3 5 7 9 10 8 6 4 2

Printed in China

Paper used in the production of this book is a natural, recyclable product made
from wood grown in sustainable forests. The manufacturing process conforms
to the environmental regulations of the country of origin

# MOLE HILL

One bright day the Moles awoke
to the smell of diesel smoke.
'Oh, Daddy! Help!' Mole's children cried,
frightened of what lurked outside.

So Mole crept out and then he saw
the last thing he was hoping for:

'Oh, no!' said Mole.
'Oh, dear! Oh, shucks!'

For on Mole Hill stood
**three huge trucks!**

First was Dozer, big and yellow,
a grim and fearsome metal fellow.

The truck beside was even greater,
the rumbling orange Excavator!

Last was Loader, strong and tough,
not quite as big—but big enough!

The diggers
moved towards
Mole's mound.
They made a dreadful,
scraping sound!

'STOP RIGHT THERE!' yelled Mole.
'THIS MINUTE!

That's my home.
My kids are in it!'

The three enormous trucks stopped still
and stared at Mole upon his hill.

'A mole can't tell us what to do.
We're a million times as big as you!
Now move aside! You're in our way.
We want to build a mall today!'

Mole stood his ground and rubbed his head,
then thinking fast, he bravely said,

'I may be smaller than a digger,
but I've faced creatures much, much bigger.'

The trucks all laughed, 'Bigger than us?'

'Bizarre!'

'Absurd!'

'Ridiculous!'

Mole smiled, 'Dig here and soon you'll see the bones of my last enemy.'

So Excavator scooped some ground
and took a look at what she'd found.

The skull of a terrific beast,
a hundred feet from west to east!
The creature's neck was very long.
Its tree-trunk legs were thick and strong.

Then Dozer pushed some dirt away
and found beneath, to his dismay,
a massive skull, a bony plate,
and two great horns, both long and straight.

A third sharp spike upon the snout,
a fearsome body, broad and stout!

Loader dug in deep and slow,
down into the earth below.

He found two pairs of dreadful claws
and then, much worse, the creature's jaws!
So many teeth, all sharp as pins,
not just for smiling monstrous grins.

'These bones,' they said, 'are terrifying!
We thought, brave Mole, that you were lying.
These creatures must have reached the sky!
Now tell us, please, how did they die?'

# SHOPPING MALL

'These creatures,' said the clever Mole,
'once tried to build upon my hole.
And when they wouldn't leave my mound,
they ended up here in the ground!'

The trucks all trembled. No one blinked.

'And now,' said Mole, 'they're all . . .

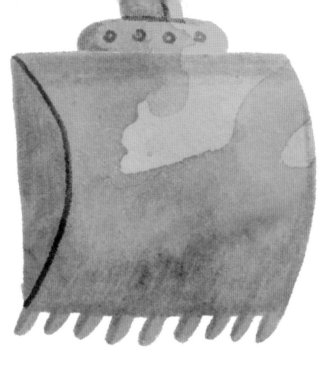

EXTINCT!'

'Oh dear! Oh no!' said Excavator.
'We're out of here! We'll see you later.'

And off they thundered down the hill.

Who knows?
They might be
running still!

At last Mole Hill was safe and sound,
so too Mole's children underground.

That night at home, the young moles said,
as Daddy tucked them into bed,
'How did the dinos really die?
We think you may have told a lie.

Our book here says they were destroyed
by an enormous asteroid!'

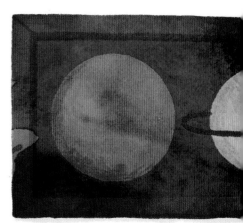

'That's true,' said Mole, 'your book is right,
a rock from space hit Earth one night.
The dust and smoke blocked out the sun.
And the days of dinosaurs were done.

But I had to scare those trucks away
So we could live another day.'

Mole leant in low and kissed each kid
and whispered softly as he did,

'No new mall, no excavator,
no rock from space or impact crater.
Not one thing, I guarantee,
will ever separate us three.'